D0102317

This Walker book belongs to:

Baghdad
PERSIA
Basra
Persian Gulf
ARABIA
Arabian Sea
AL HIN
Abyssinia
AFRICA
Indian Ocean

Sea of Pearls
Bay of Bengal
SIAM
South China Sea
SERENDIB
AL ZABAG

For Carola and Peter

First published 1994 by Walker Books Ltd
87 Vauxhall Walk, London SE11 5HJ

This edition published 2010

10 9 8 7 6 5 4 3 2 1

This book has been typeset in Calligraphic 810

Printed in China

British Library Cataloguing in Publication Data:
a catalogue record for this book is available from the British Library

ISBN 978-1-4063-1944-6

www.walker.co.uk

Sinbad the Sailor

retold and illustrated by

Marcia Williams

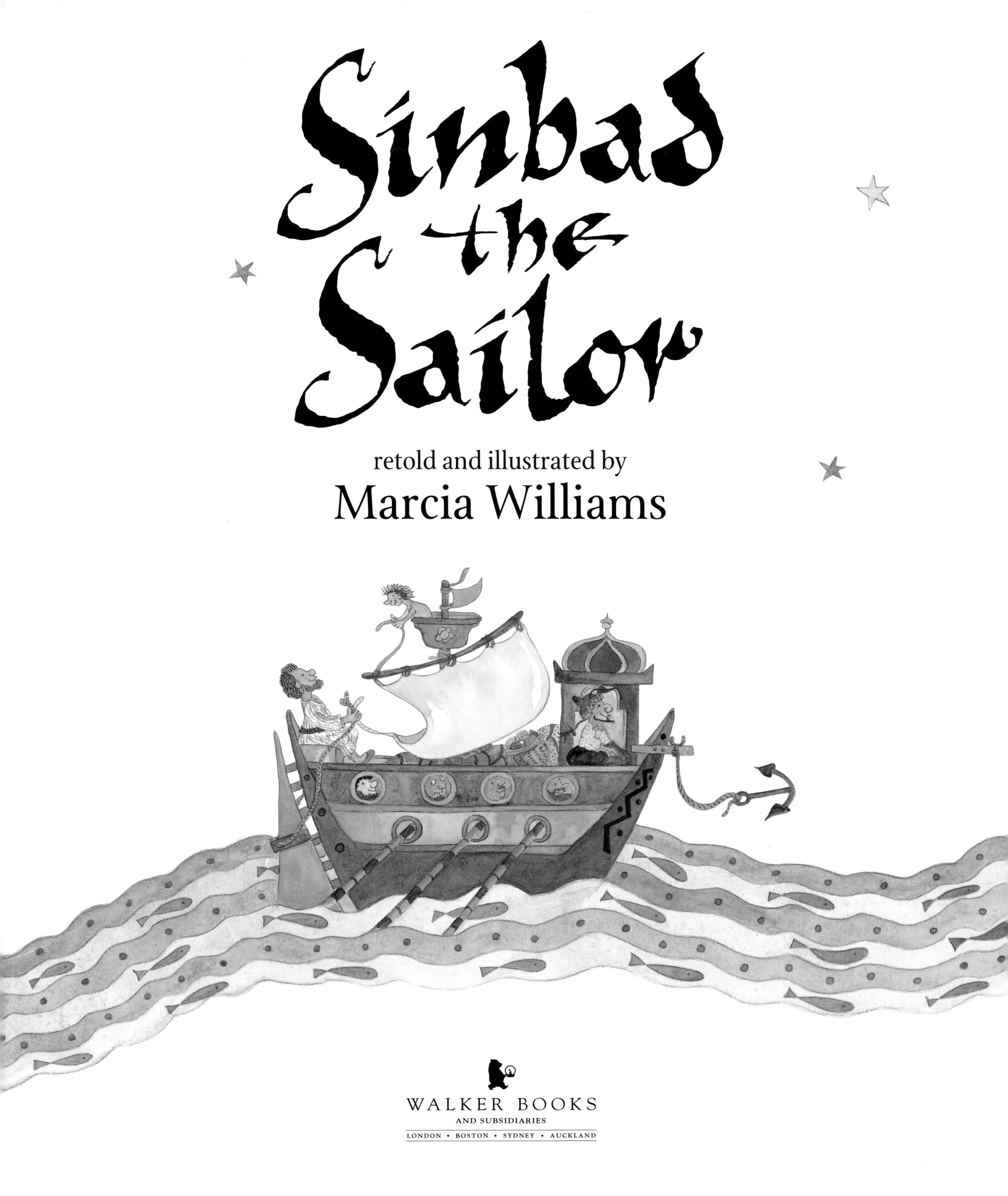

WALKER BOOKS
AND SUBSIDIARIES
LONDON • BOSTON • SYDNEY • AUCKLAND

What me? Poor, discontented? No! I just love being a pack horse to the rich. Neigh!
Me too.
Long ago, in Baghdad, there lived a poor, discontented man named Sinbad the Porter.
I'm not only weary and cross, I'm hot as well.
Me too.
One day, weary and cross from carrying his heavy load,
I hate happy people.
Me too.
the Porter sat down to rest outside a rich merchant's home.
Most of all I hate rich happy people.
Me too.
As he sat there, grumbling about the unfairness of life,
Of course, I think some rich, happy people are very nice.
He has enough food, he won't eat you!
the wealthy merchant, who had overheard him, sent out a page. The page took Sinbad the Porter by the hand and led him up the path and into the house.
It was the smell of food that carried my tongue away.
Mine too.
Anyone with the same name as mine is most welcome.
He's got the true smell of the streets.
There, the elderly merchant, Sinbad the Sailor, sat feasting with his noble friends. The Porter was overwhelmed by such grandeur, but he was made welcome and invited to share the feast.

As they ate, Sinbad the Sailor started to tell them how he had acquired his great wealth:
What a handsome fellow!
You're too kind.
"Many years ago, when I was younger and thinner,
Good old Dad.
my father died, leaving me an enormous fortune.
I really would prefer plain boiled fish.
I spent the money foolishly on exotic food and clothes.
One fish is all that's left.
How stomach-rending.
What? No cheese?
By Allah, if I'm not careful I could end up a porter, scrabbling for a living on the streets.
My legs can't dance on fish.
Then, one morning, I woke in a panic realizing that I had very little wealth left and that if I wasn't careful I would spend my old age in poverty.
Joining the workers, Sinbad?
You've got a lot to learn, mate.
You'll never sell that lot, Sinbad.
So I determined to go to sea and make my fortune. Having sold my few remaining possessions, I went to the market and bought merchandise.
This I put aboard a ship just setting sail to Basra.

SINBAD'S FIRST VOYAGE
"We left the port of Basra with our ship well loaded. Through night
and day we sailed, bartering our goods from land to land until, at last,
we reached an island as fair as the Garden of Eden.
Call me when it's ready.
Here's more wood.
I can taste you already.
Blow harder, boy.
I might find someone to trade with.
Someone like me?
Once ashore, I set off to explore while my friends built a fire.
By Allah, it's no island!
Did I blow too hard?
Baaaa! Out of the frying pan and into the sea!
Is it an earthquake?
I didn't even snap my jaws!
Suddenly the island started shaking, and the captain yelled:

All aboard!
What a view!
'This is no island. It's a whale, and you've woken it up with your fire!'
Can't even be an island in peace these days, vandals!
I'm a freshwater fish, really.
The whale dived beneath the waters.
Being a poor porter would be better than this.
You'll drown down here.
Engulfed by the sea, I was close to drowning, but I grabbed some wood
Captain... wait for me!
I love a good death.
I smell toes.
Me too.
and paddled after the ship. Alas, it sailed on, and I resigned myself to death.
For a night and a day I drifted, lashed by the wind and the waves.

"As luck would have it, I was washed ashore onto a wooded island.
I lay exhausted until the morning sun roused me.
My poor feet were swollen from many fish bites,
A sailor's lot is not a happy one.
but, cutting myself a staff, I hobbled off to explore.
I soon came upon a beautiful mare tethered to a tree and
You call this guarding?
guarded by a well-armed but sleepy groom.
The king has many horses.
He told me that the mare belonged to King Mahraza.
With teeth this big...
I'm glad I am a poor groom!
Just as I was telling him of my great adventure,
Was it you who bit my feet?
the mare started screaming. Turning towards her, we saw a sea horse trying to drag the mare into the ocean. We rushed to save her and by yelling and waving with great energy, we managed to drive the sea horse away.

Fish bites or bunions, which is worse?
"The groom then took me to King Mahraza's beautiful palace.
He was very brave.
It was nothing.
On hearing how I had helped to save his fine mare,
All this is yours to command.
the delighted king made me Controller of Shipping,
This house is yours, too.
and heaped many magnificent treasures upon me.
Oh, for just a whiff of those Baghdad streets.
In spite of his great kindness, I longed to return home.
It can't be.
It can be!
It can't be.
It can be!
So you can imagine my delight when, one joyous day,
IT IS!
the ship arrived on which I had originally set sail.
OK. You can put me down now.
It had the very same captain and all my valuable goods,
You are too kind, Sinbad.
from which I chose several fine gifts for the kindly king.
You are too kind, King Mahraza.
He, in return, gave me yet more sparkling presents
I'll miss you.
and wished me a safe and trouble-free homeward journey.
Home sweet home!
After many days' sailing, I arrived once more at Baghdad.
Here's my shopping list, and don't dawdle!
No, Your Richness.
6 Houses
10 Farms
1000 Slaves
60 Musicians
200 Turbans
10 Dancers
900 Horses
There I bought lavish houses and rich farmland.
Eat and drink but don't mention the sea.
I entertained my friends with the best food and wine.
Well, of course, when I was at sea.
Sounds fishy!
But eventually I began to forget the dangers of my voyage
I'll just go down to the docks.
Let's call him Sinbad the Sailor. Ho! Ho! Ho!
and long, once more, for the excitement of travelling at sea.
Do you believe him?
Take this gold, and come back tomorrow.
See you tomorrow.
I can't wait to tell the wife; we can earn more listening than portering!
Me too.
That is the story of my first voyage.
Tomorrow, if Allah wills it, I shall tell you the tale of my second voyage – which, although you will find it hard to believe, was even more amazing.

SINBAD'S SECOND VOYAGE

"Once again I set sail from Basra with other merchants.

From port to port we bartered our merchandise,

until we reached an uninhabited island, where we landed.

Leaving my companions, I went off to find a shady spot.

Having eaten my lunch, I settled down to sleep.

When I awoke, I realized that I was all alone, and that my ship was fast disappearing over the horizon.

Quickly I climbed a tall tree and surveyed the island.

All I could see was a strange white object in the distance.

So I made my way across the island to investigate.

It was a huge white thing, without windows or doors, at least fifty paces around and too smooth to climb. While I stood puzzling over it, the sky suddenly became as dark as night.

for the roc snatched up a large serpent and flew off almost at once. I was left to gaze in awe at a valley studded with diamonds and crawling with deadly snakes. I could see no escape.

I'll be quite cosy once I move this boulder.
"Luckily I found a cave to rest in that night,
Touch my eggs and you're dead meat.
although even there I was not entirely safe.
Good morning, world. I'm still here!
Next morning, as I emerged into the sunlight,
Or should I say: bad morning?
I tripped over a diamond-studded hunk of meat.
This smells worse than roc's leg.
In desperation I decided to secure myself to it,
Here, birdie, breakfast time...
hoping that a hungry bird would carry me to safety.
I waited nervously until a great vulture swooped down
and grabbed the meat. I was lifted high above the valley.
As the vulture landed with a jolt upon the mountain, men came screaming in from all directions, scaring the bird so much that it flew off, leaving its breakfast behind. The men were alarmed to see me tied to the meat.
We threw the meat down.
They're ours.
You can have the stinking carcass.
Diamonds or death?
It's the only way to get diamonds.
For he's a clever fellow.
They would have killed me if I had not given them the diamonds embedded in it. They then congratulated me on being the first man to come out of the valley alive, and offered to guide me home.

"We journeyed together for many days and many nights, our route taking us over rough land and tumultuous seas.

We stopped only to sell our diamonds and the other goods we had bought during our long and profitable journey.

As we travelled, we saw several truly amazing sights. Strangest of all were the rhinoceroses grazing beneath the camphor trees. They were taller than camels and their single horn was shaped in the likeness of a man.

When we finally reached Baghdad and I parted from my companions, I was a wealthy man once more.

I was able to share my good fortune with my family and friends. After some time, however, the sea called to me again.

That is the story of my second voyage.
Tomorrow, if Allah wills it, I shall tell you the tale of my third voyage – which, although you will find it hard to believe, was even more amazing.

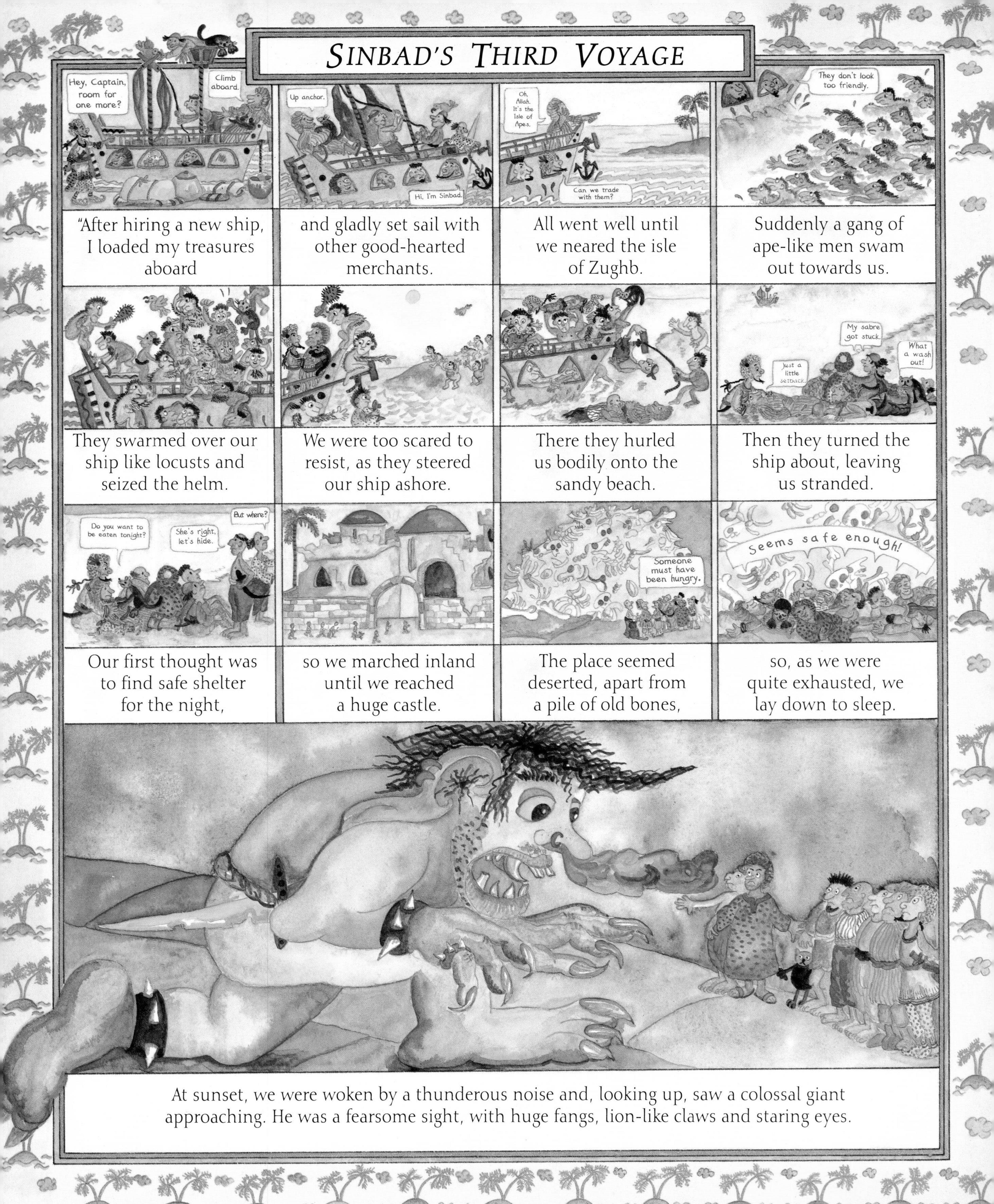
SINBAD'S THIRD VOYAGE
Hey, Captain, room for one more?
Climb aboard.
"After hiring a new ship, I loaded my treasures aboard
Up anchor.
Hi, I'm Sinbad.
and gladly set sail with other good-hearted merchants.
Oh, Allah. It's the Isle of Apes.
Can we trade with them?
All went well until we neared the isle of Zughb.
They don't look too friendly.
Suddenly a gang of ape-like men swam out towards us.
They swarmed over our ship like locusts and seized the helm.
We were too scared to resist, as they steered our ship ashore.
There they hurled us bodily onto the sandy beach.
My sabre got stuck.
What a wash out!
Just a little setback.
Then they turned the ship about, leaving us stranded.
Do you want to be eaten tonight?
She's right, let's hide.
But where?
Our first thought was to find safe shelter for the night,
so we marched inland until we reached a huge castle.
Someone must have been hungry.
The place seemed deserted, apart from a pile of old bones,
Seems safe enough!
so, as we were quite exhausted, we lay down to sleep.
At sunset, we were woken by a thunderous noise and, looking up, saw a colossal giant approaching. He was a fearsome sight, with huge fangs, lion-like claws and staring eyes.

Escaping from the giant was harder than we imagined, for he was most unwilling to let his larder of food sail away, and even brought his wife to attack us. All but myself and two others were killed.

You're safe with me.
I'll even feed you.
Well, at least we won't be eaten alive.
"For a night and a day we drifted. At last, we were cast up on another island.
This seems a safe spot.
Hungry and exhausted, we lay down to sleep.
I thought it was warm.
When we awoke, we found ourselves encircled by a great serpent,
which suddenly grabbed one of my friends
YUM!
and swallowed him whole!
I'll be back.
Everyone's eaten but us.
It then glided off, leaving us grief-stricken and afraid.
It won't find us up here.
That's for sure.
The next evening we hid in the top branches of a tree.
HISS
HISS
But as night fell, we heard the snake's hissing grow closer ...
YUM
YUM
and closer until, in a flash, my friend vanished.
I'd rather
kill myself
than be
eaten alive!
Descending the tree at daybreak, I went to drown myself.
While there's
life
there's hope!
But my courage failed. So I built a box to hide in.
HISS!
HISS!
HISS
All night long, as I lay inside, I heard the snake.
Bother.
Yet when morning came and I peeped out, it had gone.
I'm here.
Help!
Please.
Hurry.
Allah be praised!
As I walked along the beach, wondering how to escape, I saw a ship in the distance.
Grabbing a branch, I waved and shouted until the ship changed direction
and started heading towards me.

You won't be eating me for supper tonight!
"It was with great joy that I sailed away from that fearful island.
Time for a change of clothes, Sinbad.
The captain was a kindly fellow. He fed and clothed me
The new me!
Smells sweeter.
Looks finer.
Lasts longer.
and, little by little, I regained my strength.
Don't I recognize you?
Imagine my delight on realizing that I was aboard the ship
You left me to die!
that had sailed off and left me on the Isle of the Roc!
But I forgive you, as my cargo is still here.
All my precious cargo was still on board.
As we sailed on from island to island,
It's killing me to bring it to you at this price.
A likely story.
I was able to trade, and I made a very pleasing profit,
I'm rich again.
Me too.
so that when we reached Basra I was rich again.
I hope they've got the home fires burning.
I boarded a boat travelling up river to Baghdad,
It's party time again.
where my friends had gathered to give me a riotous welcome.
Everyone's invited, even those too poor to dress!
I'm too poor to dress.
I willingly shared my wealth with rich and poor alike,
I believe I can smell the sea.
You're Sinbad the Sailoring again.
until my restless soul once more cried out for the sea.
You have to admire the man.
Take this gold, and come back tomorrow.
See you tomorrow.
Ambition certainly has its dangers.
Best to be poor at home.
That is the story of my third voyage.
Tomorrow, if Allah wills it, I shall tell you the tale of my fourth voyage – which, although you will find it hard to believe, was even more amazing.

SINBAD'S FOURTH VOYAGE

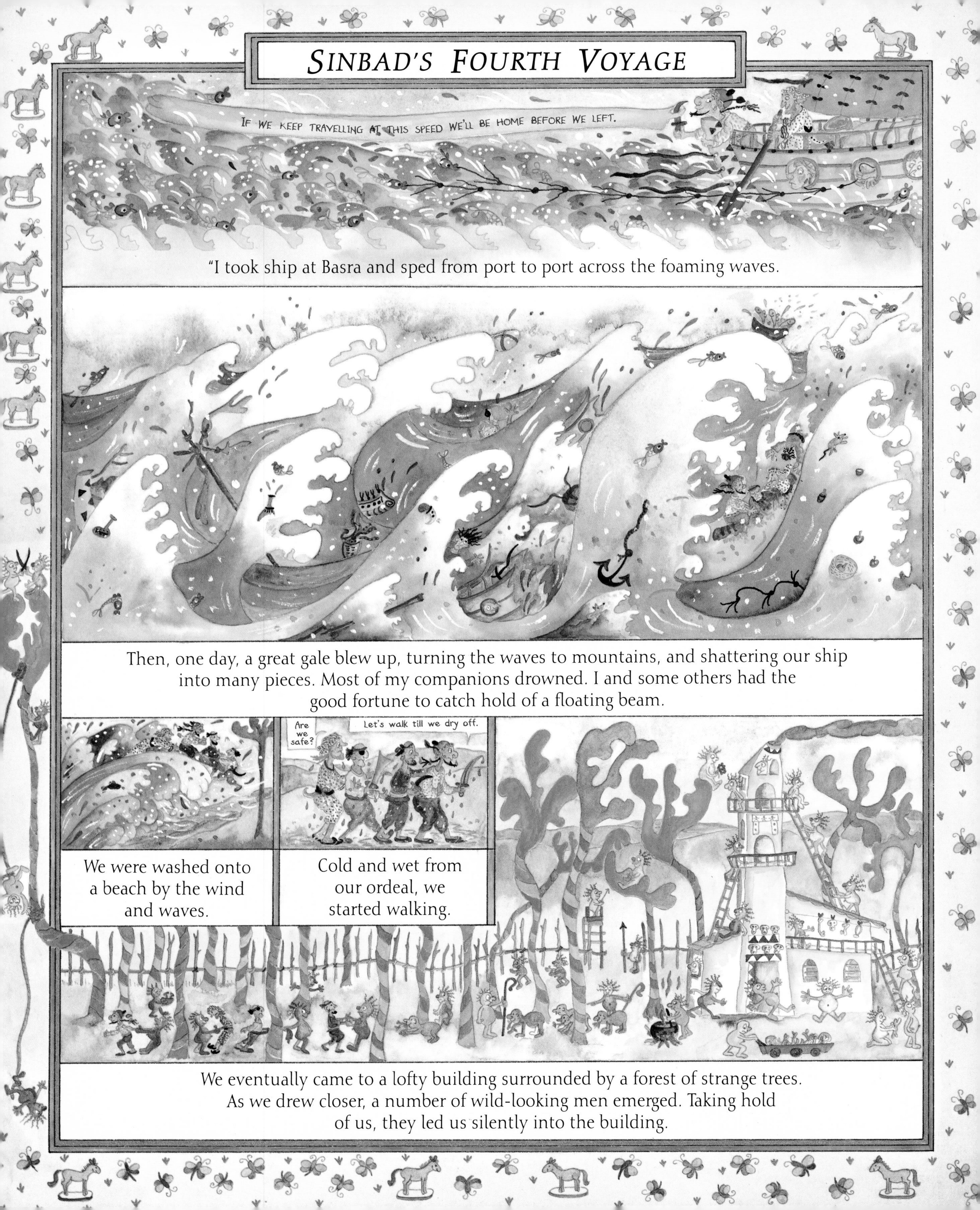

"I took ship at Basra and sped from port to port across the foaming waves.

Then, one day, a great gale blew up, turning the waves to mountains, and shattering our ship into many pieces. Most of my companions drowned. I and some others had the good fortune to catch hold of a floating beam.

We were washed onto a beach by the wind and waves.

Cold and wet from our ordeal, we started walking.

We eventually came to a lofty building surrounded by a forest of strange trees. As we drew closer, a number of wild-looking men emerged. Taking hold of us, they led us silently into the building.

"Inside, their king was seated on his throne.
How kind.
He called for food and ordered us to sit and eat.
Sorry, too much excitement.
My stomach revolted at the sight of food.
MUNCH
GOBBLE
But my friends fell upon the feast, guzzling ravenously.
MORE
MORE
MORE
MORE
The more they ate, the more they seemed to want.
GUZZLE
BURP
YUM
YUM
BURP
BURP
As they stuffed themselves, their stomachs grew
OINK
MOO
BAA
and their brains shrank. They became as beasts.
I doubt if even your brains would be juicy.
They're only sawdust, Your Majesty.
I knew then that the king of this island was a cannibal!
We'll have them for our wedding feast, Petal.
He was fattening up my friends ready for a feast!
Smell that grass!
They were led away to be pastured in a field.
Anyone for spare-ribs?
As I had eaten nothing and was only skin and bone,
the cannibals lost interest in me and I was able to escape.
Are you friendly?
Terribly.
After walking for eight days, I met some peasants,
We only eat guests on Sundays!
who took me by boat to a neighbouring isle.
Eat you? I'd have to fatten you up a bit first!
Your bones would do me.
The king of this island was a charming vegetarian.
How come you are all so rich?
It's just more fun that way.
It was a prosperous place, with many beautiful horses,
Only trouble is, we're not sure how to stay on!
but not one person had ever heard of a saddle,
Bother!
Sinbad, you're a genius!
so I made a very beautiful one for the king.
A small reward.
But not too small!
Delighted with his gift, he gave me jewels galore,
SINBAD THE SADDLER
You promised.
I'm next.
Me.
No, me.
and I became a happy and wealthy saddle maker.

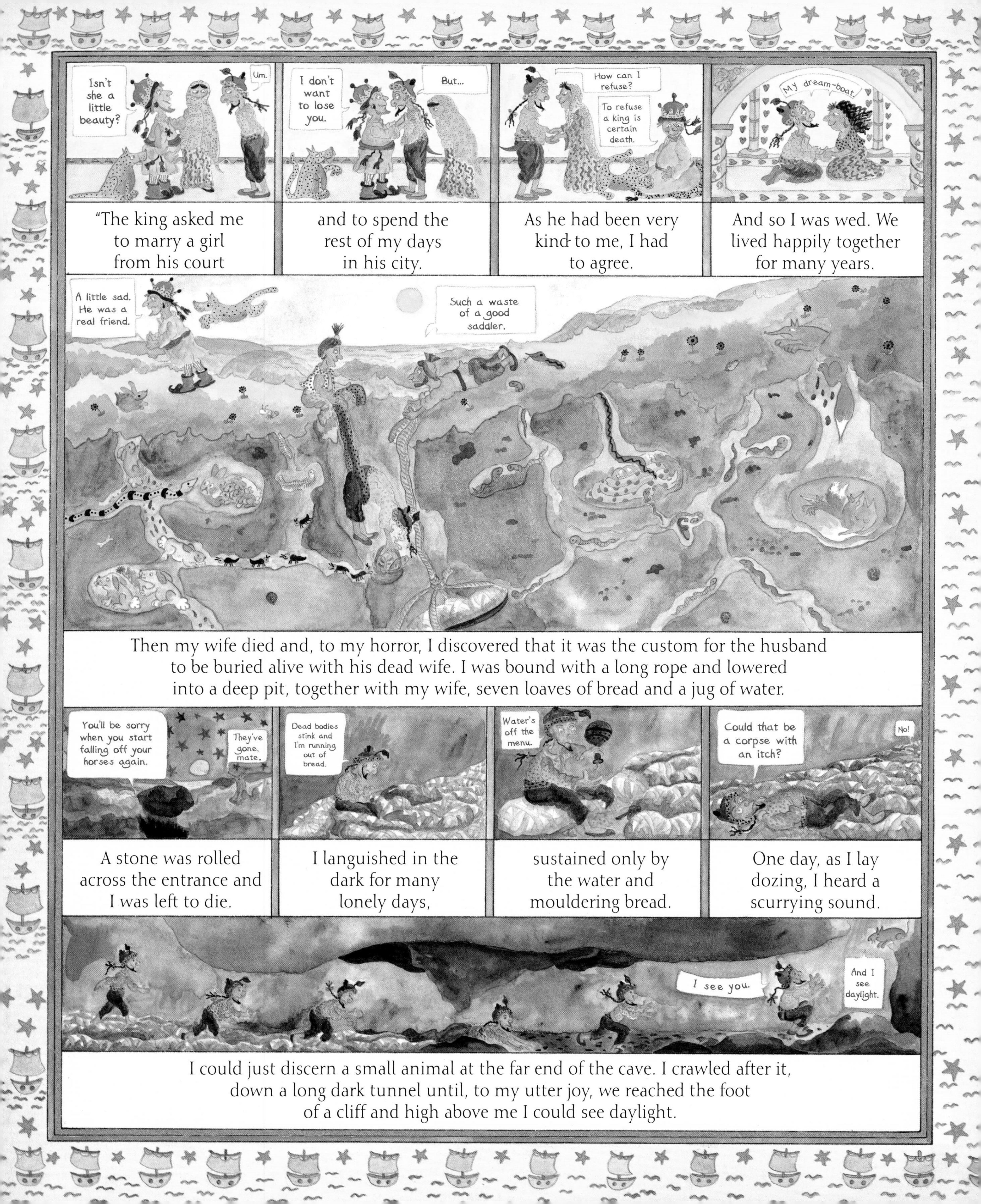
Isn't she a little beauty?
Um.
"The king asked me to marry a girl from his court
I don't want to lose you.
But...
and to spend the rest of my days in his city.
How can I refuse?
To refuse a king is certain death.
As he had been very kind to me, I had to agree.
My dream-boat.
And so I was wed. We lived happily together for many years.
A little sad. He was a real friend.
Such a waste of a good saddler.
Then my wife died and, to my horror, I discovered that it was the custom for the husband to be buried alive with his dead wife. I was bound with a long rope and lowered into a deep pit, together with my wife, seven loaves of bread and a jug of water.
You'll be sorry when you start falling off your horses again.
They've gone, mate.
A stone was rolled across the entrance and I was left to die.
Dead bodies stink and I'm running out of bread.
I languished in the dark for many lonely days,
Water's off the menu.
sustained only by the water and mouldering bread.
Could that be a corpse with an itch?
No!
One day, as I lay dozing, I heard a scurrying sound.
I see you.
And I see daylight.
I could just discern a small animal at the far end of the cave. I crawled after it, down a long dark tunnel until, to my utter joy, we reached the foot of a cliff and high above me I could see daylight.

I suppose the surface is up there.
You suppose right.
"With an enormous effort, I struggled to the surface.
Freedom!
I rejoiced in the warmth of the sunshine.
Hurry, I'm starving.
I prayed to Allah that soon a ship would rescue me.
I'll swap this priceless pearl for that worthless fish.
No deal!
Meanwhile, I spent the time admiring the jewels hidden in my turban.
What's the panic, Sinbad? Don't you like it here?
Eventually I saw a ship sailing close to shore. So, unwinding my turban, I tied it to a stick and ran up and down the beach, waving it frantically. Luckily, the crew saw me and sent a small boat ashore.
After many days' sailing the ship reached the port of Basra,
I'm alive, I'm alive! Don't bury me!
I'll just turn you white overnight, then.
and although I was haunted by nightmares about the cavern,
Take these jewels and buy me 100 more slaves, 20 more dancing girls, 6 farms and 2 houses.
Old Money Bags.
I resumed my rich life – with the help of my jewels.
See how the sun glistens so invitingly on the water.
Will you be leaving now or in the morning?
But the day came when I forgot my terrors and longed to go to sea again.
Aren't we lucky not to have sailed with him!
Take this gold, and come back tomorrow.
See you tomorrow.
These stories make me seasick!
Nearly eaten! Buried alive! We're better off staying poor and at home!
That is the story of my fourth voyage.
Tomorrow, if Allah wills it, I shall tell you the tale of my fifth voyage – which, although you will find it hard to believe, was even more amazing than my fourth.

SINBAD'S FIFTH VOYAGE

"I bought a fine ship with captain and crew and, having loaded her with merchandise, set sail. I traded with people of many lands before we came to an island where we caught sight of a roc's egg.

My passengers went ashore to view this wonder but, not content with just looking, they began throwing stones. Alas, the egg was soon broken, revealing a chick inside, which my foolish friends plucked, cooked and ATE!

Horrified at what they had done, I got them aboard and weighed anchor as quickly as possible. Unfortunately, not quickly enough, for soon the world about us grew dark, as the gigantic rocs arrived to take their revenge.

The huge birds aimed such large boulders at us that great chasms opened in the sea. Finally, they scored a direct hit upon my ship, crushing many of my crew and hurling others into the sea to be swallowed by the waves.

Oh, that's it! No more voyages for me!
That was a turban-raising event.
"I alone managed to save myself by climbing into a piece of wreckage. Aided by the wind and current, I at length reached a beautiful island where I rested on the beach until I had recovered my strength.
What a peaceful place.
I then set off to look for food along the bank of a brook.
O venerable Sheikh.
As I strolled along, I met an old man clad in leaves.
O great survivor!
Thinking he, too, was a shipwrecked mariner, I smiled;
but he only indicated he wished to be carried across the stream.
Never give a lift to a strange bunny.
My good deed for the day!
Bending low, I lifted him onto my back, but when we reached the other side he refused to get down. Desperately I tried to shake him off, but he wound his hairy legs around me tighter and tighter and I fell senseless to the ground.
Death by roc would be better than this.
Maybe I should put him out of his misery.
No. Why spoil the fun?
When I recovered, the old man was still clinging fast to my back. He kicked me until I was forced to rise and walk with him. For weeks I carried him everywhere. I longed for Death to release me.

I wish this was poison, but wine will dull the senses, at least.
"One day I squeezed some grape juice into an empty gourd.
Mmm, a vintage year.
After several days in the sun it had turned into wine,
You are a great fat hairy baboon!
and when I drank some it gave me fresh vigour.
Don't feel shy, just help yourself.
Seeing the effect on me, the old man demanded some.
He's going.
He soon became light-headed and relaxed his grip,
He's going.
so, with a violent shake, I hurled him to the ground
HE'S GONE!
and then hit him on the head with a great rock.
Free to roam wherever I will.
Well, almost.
Overjoyed to be free, I roamed about the island.
Not even paddling is safe these days!
Some weeks later, I saw a ship approach.
Real people!
I ran to meet the passengers as they came ashore.
You must be Sinbad the Superman.
The very same.
They were astounded by my escape from the old man
He has strangled many sailors with his hairy thighs.
Ug!
who, they told me, was the Old Man of the Sea.
They took me aboard their ship and we sailed away
to the City of Apes, perched high on a cliff.
What does a merchant with no goods do?
Mmm, that's a poser.
There I went in search of employment.
My friends will show you.
I was introduced to a couple of youths with sacks of stones,
What I need is a porter.
given a sack, and told to follow them.
Eventually we came to a coconut grove full of monkeys,
who climbed to the treetops as we approached.
Copying the others, I began hurling stones at these monkeys.

"The furious monkeys retaliated by hurling coconuts at us. These we gathered until our sacks bulged.
Hand-picked coconuts for sale!
Lovely milk for the kiddies.
Let me show you our finest selection.
We then returned to the city and sold the coconuts for an excellent profit. I did this several times.
HOME!
Soon I could afford my passage back to Basra.
Come on, Captain, treat yourself to a Sinbad Special.
How can I resist?
On the way, I was able to sell more coconuts,
and when we reached the Sea of Pearls
I hired several skilled divers to work for me.
I think I can afford a small bonus.
In a short time I had a hoard of priceless pearls,
One more, Captain, then I'll have enough for a new house!
HIC!
so, once more, I was returning a rich man.
Anything for us?
On reaching home I was greeted by my friends.
Give one pearl to every poor child you meet.
I shared my wealth with them and the poor.
Shall we tell what happened in the China Seas?
No!
Well I'll go there myself, anyway.
Back to the kitchen. He's off to sea again!
I lived a delightful life of ease until I made the mistake of entertaining a group of adventurers, who reminded me of the pleasures and excitement of travelling the high seas. And so I felt the urge, eventually, to leave home once again.
Makes our lives seem as dull as mud.
Take this gold, and come back tomorrow.
See you tomorrow.
See you tomorrow, Spotty.
Wealth seems somewhat overrated to me.
Me too.
That is the story of my fifth voyage.
Tomorrow, if Allah wills it, I shall tell you the story of my sixth voyage – which, although you will find it hard to believe, was even more amazing.

SINBAD'S SIXTH VOYAGE

"Having set sail from Basra with a rich cargo, we voyaged leisurely for a time, remembering all the strange and wonderful things we had seen on other voyages.

One day, in mid-ocean, the captain burst into a loud lament, as the ship had been driven into unknown and dangerous waters. Just as we were turning about ...

a great wind arose, dashing our ship upon the rocks. Many of my companions were drowned, but others, like myself, clung to the rocks and dragged themselves ashore.

The sands were littered with other wrecks and their valuable cargo, and the whole place was lit up by a jewel-encrusted river which flowed into a dark cavern.

"There seemed no way to escape and the days dragged by as we waited for our food to run out and then death. One by one I buried my companions, until I alone was left.

I began to dig myself a grave in which to lie as death approached. But as I dug, I began to think that every river must have a beginning and an end, so I made myself a raft from aloe wood.

Having loaded it with sacks of gems and ambergris, I launched myself upon the river. The current tossed me from side to side, carrying me deep into the cavern's darkness.

He's a goner.

As the passage narrowed, I was forced onto my belly. Faster and faster I was swept along until, overcome by fear, I fell into a death-like sleep.

"I awoke to find myself close to a bank and surrounded by Indians and Abyssinians. They brought me food and, with the help of one who could speak Arabic, I told my story.

They then formed a long procession and carried me and my cargo to their king, Serendib, so that he, too, could marvel at my adventure and lucky escape.

The king greeted me warmly and listened in astonishment to my tale. He was delighted when I presented him with some of the finest jewels I had collected on the beach.

He invited me to be his guest and we spent many happy hours discussing the merits of each others' country and method of government.

"So impressed was the king by my stories of the wise Caliph of Baghdad, that he asked me if I would take gifts and a letter to this great monarch. I was pleased to comply.

The king himself arranged for my passage and loaded me with many gifts for the Caliph and myself and so I bade farewell to my many friends on that agreeable island.

We reached Basra safely and went from there to Baghdad and the Caliph's palace. He was amazed by the splendour of the gifts sent by the king and by my strange adventure.

After this, I firmly resolved to stay at home. But then one day, while I was visiting the Caliph, he said that the time had come for me to carry his presents to King Serendib.

That is the story of my sixth voyage.
Tomorrow, if Allah wills it, I shall tell you the story of my seventh voyage – which, although you will find it hard to believe, was even more amazing.

Sinbad's Seventh Voyage

"Most unwillingly, I set sail for the island of Serendib with the Caliph's letter and a cargo of gifts. The journey took two long months but we finally arrived without mishap.

The king was overjoyed to see me and to be honoured so by the Caliph. He wanted me to stay with him but I was anxious to return home to Baghdad, so only stayed long enough to reload.

We journeyed home peacefully for many days. Then a sudden tempest hit the ship, drenching our cargo with rain. As we struggled to cover it, a terrible roar rose from the sea.

Looking about, we saw a great sea monster rushing towards us. It seized our ship in its vast jaws and as I dived off the side it swallowed it down in one gulp.

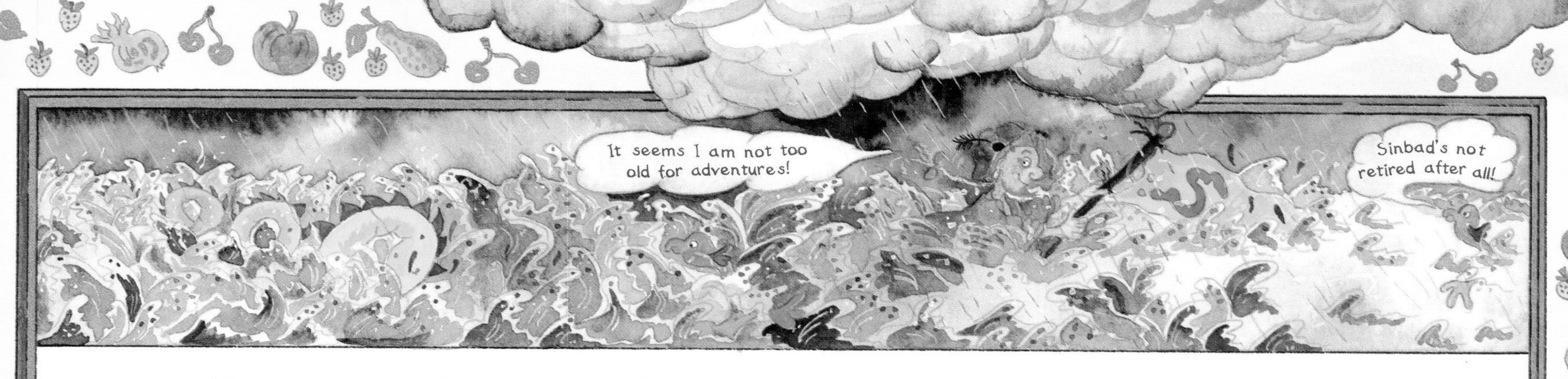

"The monster sank beneath the foaming ocean and I was left alone, clinging to a piece of timber. For two days and two nights I battled against the stormy weather ...

until I was cast upon an island covered with fruit trees and watered by many streams. I wandered about until I came to a fast-flowing river which I resolved to travel down by raft.

I made a sturdy raft from some exotic wood and pushed off down river. I sped along on the current at great speed; faster and faster I sped until I realized I must be heading for a precipice.

Resigning myself to death, I closed my eyes. Then, as the raft reached the very edge, I felt it halt. Opening my eyes, I found I had been saved by a net thrown by some men on the bank.

He's no tiddler.
"The men hauled me over to the muddy bank.
May I be of assistance?
I lay there exhausted until an old man kindly helped me up
Hello, wrinkly.
Perfume him well.
and took me to the city baths, where I was washed.
Think of this as your home.
My pleasure.
Afterwards, he took me to his house and cared for me.
Trust nobody, Sinbad. Ever!
He even said he would help me sell my wares,
But I have nothing to trust anyone with.
which puzzled me, as I was unaware of having any.
This is not nothing!
Well crafted.
Philistine.
At the market I discovered that he meant my raft.
Call yourself a merchant? It's sandalwood!
I'll sell!
WE'LL BUY.
It was made of sandalwood and sold for a fortune.
It's fun having a friend to do things with.
Looking for us?
I stayed happily with the old man for some time.
Then you'll be like a son to me.
When he asked me to marry his beautiful daughter,
OK, Dad.
I was unable to refuse such a genial host.
You are the finest catch of all my voyages.
Luckily we grew to love each other dearly.
I'd have been a dull old man without you.
When the old man died, I inherited his wealth
This is fun, but could you teach me a slower dance now?
and continued to live happily with his daughter.
Wings! You must be joking.
It's the local flappers.
Then I found that once a year the local men grew wings
It's no joke, Sinbad.
I want to do it.
We're too young.
and for a whole day flew high above the city.
Eager to join them, I persuaded a friend to let me ride on his back. All went well until we flew so close to Heaven, that I heard the angels sing. 'Praise be to Allah,' I cried, and at once we plummeted back to earth.

I used to be a high flyer.
"Such was the force of the fall that I fainted.
Not even an echo.
I came to alone, on top of a barren mountain.
If only I was a goat.
I despaired of ever finding a way down.
I really do taste awful.
Then two boys with wands of red gold approached.
Could this be a magic wand?
One of them gave me his wand and pointed to a path.
As I rounded a rock, I bumped into a huge snake
Mind my wings!
that was in the middle of swallowing my flying friend,
so I struck the snake a deadly blow with my wand.
You shouldn't have mentioned that name.
I then learnt that the mention of 'Allah' had caused our fall.
I'm no angel, you know!
I'll never say it again!
So, promising not to mention him again, I was flown home.
Can they really be so evil that they fear the name of Allah?
All except my dad.
There I discovered these city men were the Devil's brothers,
Hurry and pack.
Don't leave me behind.
so my wife and I decided to return to my home.
Only 1000 dinars, excluding the cat and the wife.
I knew he loved me.
Having sold all our goods, we left the wicked city
Baghdad, the City of Peace. You'll love it.
Baghdad ahoy!
and sailed home to my beloved Baghdad.
Here she is. Isn't she a catch?
You old sea dog, you!
Humph!
There I introduced my wife to my dear friends
Take these dinar and buy me more of everything and even more of more for my wife.
Yes, Your Esteemed Richness.
and set about putting my house in order.
Anyone for snake with flying stuffing?
Maybe he'll join our landlubbers' club, now.
Last voyage, last good meal, I fear.
Me too.
And this is the pearl of my voyages.
Humph!
That is the story of my seventh and last voyage.
I was away from home for twenty-seven years and was certainly cured of any desire to travel abroad again."

By the time Sinbad the Sailor had told his last tale, Sinbad the Porter was a changed man.
Did I hear a "yes"?
I'd rather be a dull drudge than risk life and limb for wealth.
Me too.
Me– now!
Seems we have two happy Sinbads here.
And I'd risk life and limb a hundred times more for the smell of the sea and my treasure.
Call her a treasure?
To him, the humble life of a porter seemed more desirable than a perilous one in pursuit of wealth and power.
Sinbad the Sailor
invites you to a feast in honour of Sinbad the Porter.
Cheers to us Sinbads.
I love a good feast.
Eat up, SP.
Strange taste.
Roc's Eggflip, SP?
Music aids the digestion.
Do dance and eat.
Can you guess why seven?
Do reach up for more.
Nine days of eating is filling.
Speak for your-selves.
Are you full yet, SP?
No, no, no!
Roast sea cow, then?
Or juggled fruit?
I expect you're full, now.
Almost half full.
Still feasting?
Trumpet music is filling.
A game of chess might be fun.
Yum.
I'm not sure the board was edible.
I'm half full now.
Me too.
We'll drink to that.
My wife will make some tea.
I should have more room soon.
Twenty days of fun.
Then try an egg.
Actually, SS, I fancy something sweet.
Me too.
Bring on the puds!
I'm nearly full now, SS.
Me too.
Does that mean we can go home?
Maybe just one last plum.
Or even two.
I do hate waste.
It's just a plum stone.
Wake up, he's full. You can go.
Three cheers for SS and good night to you.
And good night to us.
To celebrate Sinbad the Porter's wisdom, Sinbad the Sailor gave a magnificent feast that lasted thirty days and thirty nights.

Sinbad the Sailor and Sinbad the Porter vowed to remain friends.

Thereafter, they spent many happy hours together, playing with their model ships and discussing the wonders and terrors of Sinbad the Sailor's seven amazing voyages.

Baghdad
PERSIA
Basra
Persian Gulf
ARABIA
Arabian Sea
AL HIN
Abyssinia
AFRICA
Indian Ocean